AuthorHouse™ UK
1663 Liberty Drive
Bloomington, IN 47403 USA
www.authorhouse.co.uk
Phone: 0800.197.4150

Published by AuthorHouse 01/18/2016

ISBN: 978-1-4389-1264-6 (sc)

Print information available on the last page.

authorHOUSE®

Hailey's MAGIC STONE

Joy Allman

Illustrated by Marie Delderfield

It was Thursday morning and Mrs Miller was in the classroom preparing work for the children.

"Hi Miss" said Hailey, she was the first child to arrive.
"Look what I've got!" Hailey held her cupped hands underneath her teacher's nose, "its magic" she said with a beaming smile.

"Good morning Hailey, "what's magic?" asked Mrs Miller.
 "My stone, its magic!" answered Hailey unfolding her fingers to give her teacher a closer look.

Mrs Miller stopped what she was doing to look closer at Hailey's stone, "Oh yes, how pretty, with all those lovely colours, would you like to show the class after the register?" she asked.

Hailey sat up straight with her arms tightly folded and feeling rather important while Mrs Paterson called the register.

Mrs Miller gave the stone to Mrs Paterson who held it out for the children to see and said, "Hailey has brought in something special to show us".

"Wow Wee!" said Fatima; "Yes it is a beautiful stone" agreed Mrs Paterson, "I can see why Hailey wanted to show and tell, would you like to tell the class how you got it?"

"Bobby, the shopkeeper gave it to me, she told me she found it but did not know what to do with it. "Bobby said I should look after it because it's magic!" Hailey explained in a proud voice.

"Magic, wow!" said Iqbal. Just then Hailey noticed Mrs Miller smile and wink at Mrs Paterson, "they don't believe my stone is *really* magic" she thought sadly.

"Ok Hailey, thank you for showing us your stone" said Mrs Miller, "put it in your pocket and you can let the children have a closer look at playtime".

At playtime Hailey's friends wanted to see her stone again.
"Let's see if it's *really* magic! What does it do?" quizzed Fatima excitedly.

Hailey did not **really** know if the stone was magical, she was so excited when Bobby gave it to her; she just took it '*no questions asked!*

Hailey couldn't honestly answer Fatima's question, so she just said "Err yes, let's sit in a circle then we can pass it around"!

"I know" let's all make a wish when it's our turn to hold the stone" said Fatima.

Hailey smiled at Fatima's idea and became excited as each child made their wish. When it was Hailey's turn to make her wish, she held her stone and closed her eyes and in a loud and excited voice she said,

"I-wish-I-didn't-have-to-go-back-to-class-to-do-work-I-wish-I-was-somewhere-far-away-doing-something-fun-and-exciting!"

All of a sudden Hailey felt something almost unexplainable, strange and possibly *magical* happening. "Wowwaahh" sounded Hailey as she felt herself spinning and then suddenly stopping with a **bump**!

"Wow what happened?" Hailey said rubbing her eyes and expecting a reply from her friends, but as she opened her eyes she realised there were **no friends; No playground; NO SCHOOL in site!!**

Confused Hailey rubbed her eyes again "where am I, where are my friends?" she said, looking around.

The only things Hailey could see were clear blue skies and miles and miles of green fields. She stood up slowly; still finding it hard to believe her own eyes.

Hailey's tummy began to do summersaults; one minute she was in school, then in the time *space of a blink*, she was in what felt like a **big** *daydream!*

Hailey realised that she was on the top of a steep hill; all she could see was green grass and spreads of daisies and buttercups.

Poor Hailey began to worry about her friends, "they must be here somewhere, maybe they got here before me and **they're** looking for **me**", she hoped.

Hailey began to walk down the hill but it was too steep and it forced her to run down instead, this made her giggle!

The sun was shining at its brightest; Hailey stretched her arms out like an aeroplane and continued flying down the hill instead, this was fun! She thought.

After some time Hailey became tired and thirsty, she needed to rest so she sat down beside some daisies and began to think about her friends again "oh where can they be" she wondered.

Thinking of her friends Hailey remembered Fatima's question about the stone really being Magic, when she remembered! "Oh yes my stone, my **Magic** stone! Pulling her stone out of her pocket Hailey stared at it as it sparkled in the sunlight. "I knew it, you **are** magic!" Hailey said as she kissed it then safely put it back in her pocket.

Hailey smiled to herself, one of those smiles she wore when Mrs Miller had praised her for doing good class work.

Only this time she smiled because...

"I'm not in class doing work and when Mrs Miller does see me she will not be happy!"

This thought gave Hailey butterflies and at the same time made her chuckle, giggle then burst into laughter "ha-ha ha-ha". She patted her pocket checking her magic stone was safe then continued her adventure running, skipping, flying and rolling down the hill.

Hailey had been running for some time and now she could see in the distance. She could see colourful things moving around and although she was tired this filled her with a burst of energy.

As Hailey got closer she could hear music playing, and even nearer she could now see... "Yippee, a Fun Fair!"

Hailey could see babies in pushchairs eating ice creams; children on a merry-go-round; high rides, fast rides, and a candy floss hut.

Hailey's eyes lit up and her tummy rumbled.

"Hello luv", came a friendly voice as Hailey walked into the fair. Hailey looked up and saw a rather large bald headed man standing behind a counter selling candy floss, toffee apples, burgers and hot dogs.

"Have a hot dog," said the man, "No thank you sir, I'm a vegetarian" replied Hailey politely.

"No worries," said the man "we can fix that" and he gave a loud whistle to the lady serving on the opposite stall.
"Fix this young lady up a princess special Val" he shouted and pointed Hailey over to the other stall.

"There you go my luvly" said the lady handing Hailey some French fries and a large strawberry milkshake, "get that down yah" she said. Hailey got up onto a stool and tucked into her tasty yummy food!

Hailey could hear someone shouting from behind "Roll up - Roll up"; she turned around to see a short man with a little voice, calling "last call for the last ride on the spinning top!"

"I want a go" shouted Hailey excitedly, she jumped off the stool and ran over to the spinning top waving her hands excitedly in the air, "come on then little miss, step on and belt up".

When Hailey was safely strapped in, the little man pressed the big green button and Hailey held on tightly. The spinning top tilted to one side; then it spun slowly at first then it started to spin faster and faster, and then rising into the air it spun even faster "Whowwww" sounded Hailey.

Hailey was just too excited to be frightened, "whaaat a ride" she laughed nervously.

Hailey spent the whole afternoon enjoying ride after ride, she even won a giant pink balloon with little white fluffy balls inside by knocking down 5 coconuts, all by herself.

"This was the best fun ever!" she thought and again she remembered her friends and school. "This adventure would have been even better if my friends were here".

Hailey began to feel tired and sad and thinking about Mrs Miller gave her butterflies only this time it did **not** make her giggle.

So Hailey made her way out of the fun fair and back to the grassy hills holding onto her prize balloon.

Hailey remembered this was how her adventure had started as she sat on the grass with her legs crossed and again she remembered her stone!

Hailey pulled the stone out of her pocket and hugged it with both hands saying "thank you I've had a great adventure".

All of a sudden Hailey heard a fluttering sound above her head. She looked up, "oh no my balloon" she cried but she was too tired to try to catch it so she watched it fly away.

Putting the stone to her lips Hailey made another wish.

"I–wish–I–was–back-at-school–and-it-was-home-time"

Again Hailey felt a sudden spinning which stopped with a bump and in the time space of a blink...

Suddenly, Hailey found herself standing in the line with the rest of her class friends; they were stood at the classroom door waiting for the home time bell to ring.

"Hailey Pringle!" came a familiar but very cross voice of Mrs Miller who stood staring at Hailey with her arms folded. "Where on earth have you been? We have been looking everywhere for you?"

Hailey's friends stared at her too, waiting for her to answer.
 "Miss I-I c-can explain" stuttered Hailey holding her stone up at her teacher.

 Mrs Miller took the stone from Hailey, "Oh yes and it had better good young lady" she said.

Hailey knew she was in **big** trouble so she quickly she said, "Miss one minute we were in the playground and the next minute I was having a really great adventure!"

But before Hailey could barely finish her sentence Mrs Miller interrupted, **"Adventure indeed!"** Mrs Miller waved the stone in the air saying, *"I–wish-I-could -just-go–off-to-somewhere-nice–but-I..."*

...and before Mrs Miller could finish off **her** sentence, and in *the time space of a blink*, Mrs Miller **vanished** into thin air!

At first the children gasped in shock, "Uhhhh" then they started to giggle, and when Hailey burst into laughter her friends all joined in. Hailey's friends now believed that the stone *was **really magic!***

Hailey knew that Mrs Miller would have a great adventure and in the time space of a blink she would be home in time for her tea!

About the author

Joy Allman was born and grew up in the South of London, England.

Joy has spent most of her working life in child care supporting children with individual special needs, a chosen career which she throughly enjoys, she is currently pursuing a career in primary teaching. Joy enjoys travelling and in 2008 with a fear of heights she experienced her first and last! Mountain climb up the Atlas Mountains in Morocco with a dear friend. She loves listening to all kinds of music and has been writing children's stories since secondary school she has now decided to share them with you.

For my son Daniel, every day you're a fresh inspiration!

To my father and mother you have always been a pillar of strength.

Thanks to family and friends for your encouragement to move forward with this venture "thank you".

Lightning Source UK Ltd.
Milton Keynes UK
UKIC03n1334060416
271639UK00007B/16